ELUSIVE HORIZON

Yvonne Ebhodaghe

AuthorHouse™ UK Ltd.
500 Avebury Boulevard
Central Milton Keynes, MK9 2BE
www.authorhouse.co.uk
Phone: 08001974150

First published by AuthorHouse   01/07/2011

ISBN: 978-1-4567-7368-7

**Dedication to my mother
who believed in my inspiration to be a writer.**

Chapter 1

The jingling of the cowbells in a distance and easterly wind blowing like a whistle in the quite village, the rustle of leaves on the dry and dusty ground made the village look deserted. The odd shout from the herd boys tending the cows served as the only comfort near to humanity that Winnie could hear .Kneeling next to the well; she brushed her forehead to remove the sweat that was threatening to fall. She scratched under her tingling armpits, and she could feel the sticky sweat. She knew that she was not cold at all, she was nervous. Winnie held her breath for a few seconds to confirm that she could hear her own breath. As soon as she finished fetching water from the well, Winnie balanced the jerry can on top of her head. She walked gracefully from the forest that led from the well. She was glad to see the clearing leading to the village. The dust on the ground powdered her dry feet.

"Winnie! Winnie, oh dear is this girl deaf? Winnie! Ah!"

Winnie turned around dazed from the deep thought she had indulged herself in. She smiled as she saw her friend Tracy giving her a look of annoyance. Tracy gave her friend a friendly punch on the shoulder, "Honestly Winnie, you never cease to amaze me. I have been calling you for more than five minutes .but you kept on walking." Winnie smiled revealing the lovely dimples on each side of the cheek. She was a beautiful woman. Her face was round and she had a nose pointed nose. Her eyes were saucer sized and she had thick eyebrows that did not need any trimming or shaping of any kind. Her lips were thick and beautifully curved and when she smiled, they revealed white, same sized teeth. She was of middle height and she was a curvy woman who had a huge bottom and wide hips. She plaited her hair in natural neat cornrows. The whole village admired her beauty and personality. She was mild tempered and always ready to offer a smile. Tracy was not surprised at Winnie's composure amidst the questions she fired at her.

"Well-done just smile at me. Answer now. Why were you ignoring me.?"

Winnie looked at her friend sincerely and sighed, "Tracy, calm down. I did not hear you. Why would I ignore you? Anywhere where are you coming from?" Winnie inspected her friend from toe to head and frowned. She knew that her friend had no business to come out for at that time of the day. She solemnly hoped that she would not get the answer she was dreading for, but it was a bit late for that. Tracy rolled her eyes and laughed loudly "Madam Angel. You know Winnie, all our village elders like you? All of them?" Winnie looked at her friend and she felt a deep concern for her. Tracy continued feverently, "Anyway to put that mind at rest, I am coming from meeting up with Ben" Tracy did not look bothered at all, that is what worried Winnie most. Ben was popular in the village but all for the wrong reasons. He had a reputation of stealing livestock and even at the tender age of twenty, older men dreaded his presence. There were rumours that he once fought off a huge snake even though nobody confirmed it. That rumour propelled his reputation and it got worst to the point that villagers would let him get away with thefts for fear of his bravado. Winnie knew that the rumour was unfounded hence; she did not respect or condone his behaviour. She knew that Tracy deserved better. The two friends were same age mates. At twenty they had spend their lives together. Winnie knew that between the two of them Tracy was the one with the fierce attitude. Tracy had a short temper on her and she would slap any person who dared cross her path. She was shorter than Winnie and she had a long face and a nose that was flat as a pancake. Her eyes were small and slightly squinty. Her ears were a little bigger than normal therefore not proportionate to her head. She had buckteeth and her lips were extremely huge. She had wider hips than Winnie's and was proud of them as she used to say they were the " best part of my body" She always wore her hair short as she said in her own words "hair for me is not the crown of my glory".

Winnie tolerated her friend very much. She knew that Tracy could be irrational and hasty in decisions. Winnie normally cleaned the mess that Tracy made in her life though both of them did not realize it since there were used to it that it had become a tradition. Winnie though, could not help but worry about Tracy's choice in men. She knew her friend had a tasteless choice of men; she always went for those who hurt and used her.

Therefore, Winnie knew that she had to be careful with the way she would address her concern Tracy. Winnie faked a cough and stood in her tracks. She started taking the jerry can off her head and with Tracy's help, both girls managed to place it carefully on the dusty ground. Winnie took a deep breath and swallowed hard, "You were with Ben, weren't you Tracy?" Winnie studied her friends face; she could see the look of stubbornness on Tracy's face. "Tracy? Why are you doing this to yourself? You know his reputation, how can you even think of ...?"

"Please, please Winnie .Don't preach to me. I appreciate your friendship .I really think you have more problems .Do not burden yourself with mine. See you at work tomorrow if you make it". Tracy bolted off towards her house steadily leaving a trail of dust that made Winnie choke.

Winnie knew deep down in her heart that her friend was right. She had many problems in her life that she needed sorting out. She blinked hard as she thought of all the responsibility that had suddenly sprung on her in the last 8 months. The instant death of her only surviving mother had really influenced her greatly. As the only employed member of the family, she had to carry the responsibility of looking after the two younger siblings left behind by her parents. Her little salary was insufficient to feed the family. She could not trouble herself with her oldest brother, Batsi who at the age of 28 years was very irresponsible and careless with the little resources they could scramble.

Winnie sighed deeply when she thought of how Batsi's drinking and unemployment had left them with nothing after he sold everything to finance his habits and the love of girls. "Listen Winnie" Batsi would say, "I am the oldest, respect comes with that, automatically, and I will do whatever I want. Our late father told me that I am now the man of this house. If you want to voice out your opinion, please feel free to do so in your own husband's house. That little nurse job you are doing at the hospital is good enough to sponsor the whole family and eh, of course you give me beer money as usual". He would stagger out of the house leaving the younger children, Chipo who was 14 and Tommy who was 10 crying because sometimes he would turn violent towards them all. This kind of behaviour by her brother really upset Winnie. She knew that despite all this she had to be strong and carry on for her sibling's sake.

She felt a teardrop fall down on her left cheek, She quickly sniffed her nose to prevent a mucus that was threatening to drop...She wiped her forehead and lifted her jerry can on top of her head ,she balanced it gracefully as she walked home in time to prepare supper.

Gareth could not believe his ears...his older sister had borrowed his "pet", the silver Mercedes Benz that he had bought only a few weeks earlier. He looked at his mother sternly and shouted, "Mother, I am not having this. Katy can't just choose when and where she would love to borrow my car." He threw himself onto the sofa and held his head in his hands. He continued in an agonizing voice, "That car cost me 20000 us dollars. What if...."

"Enough". His mum stood up clapping her hands in his face .She kissed her teeth in a hissing way, "Who said something will happen to the car? You sound like she has crashed it already". Mrs Walter tried to calm her son down. She knew that her son had a temper on him, especially if things were not going his way, which was the case at present. Deep down in her heart, though she was bubbling with anger towards her daughter Katy.Mrs Walter always felt the challenges of raising children on her own whenever she had to deal with Katy's rebellious behaviour. Katy was the most spoilt amongst her three children. Being the youngest and 20 years old, she had an immature mentality that her family should work for her .She dropped out of university and did not like working. Mrs. Walter understood why her second and only son Gareth would be very angry with his younger sister. Unlike Katy, Gareth was the pride of the family second to the oldest girl Fran. Gareth never complained about not having a male influence in his life.Mr Walter had passed away 10 years ago from lung cancer. Poor Gareth bottled it all in. He had walked in his fathers footsteps and had become an accountant. He was nearly 32 years and was not interested in marrying or settling down. He was ladies' man, different women all the time. He never asked to go back to England, which was their home country.

They left their land 5 years before her husband's death. They had shared their passion of Africa with their children ever since they were little .Mrs. Walter ,her name Andrea ,always meditated on the past she shared with her husband Tom .Their honeymoon was in Rhodesia, now Zimbabwe and they really enjoyed the warmth they received from the people of that country. Andrea remembered the first Zimbabwean safari holiday she took her children on. They became fond of Africa and always mentioned of living there. Her husband had made the final decision of moving over because he felt the family needed a change. Money was not a problem as Tom had earned a lot of money in his 30 years of owning an accounting firm. The kids had been happy and had all gone to the local schools. Tom had suggested that the kids had to do their universities in England .All had gone to plan. The older kids completed their University and Fran had decided to stay in England and practise medicine, but Katy always made excuses when it came to education and she dropped out in the first year of her degree and from then on, she had remained adamant in her stubbornness.

She knew that she had to calm her son down before Katy arrived from wherever heaven knew she had gone. She stroked her son's blonde hair. She could see the anger blazing in his usually cool blue eyes. She felt sorrow as she could see the strict resemblance with her husband .She softly and calmly soothed her son. "I promise you, if she as much scratches your pet, I will ground her until she is married" Andrea tried to calm the situation down by adding some humour. She saw that her son was serious. She gathered herself together and went to the kitchen to get herself a cup of tea.

* * *

The music was blaring so loud that not all the clubbers could feel their heartbeats. The vibration was sending tremors through their bodies. Alcohol was flowing freely at Missy B nightclub. It was a very popular place for youngsters, not just ordinary ones, but the rich and affluent. Katy knew that is were she belonged. She showed off to her peers her cash and that she could afford the best things in life. Hence, she did not feel guilty for stealing her older brother's car. She knew she had committed the deadliest sin in comparison with Gareth's anger .Lest she did not care.

She straightened her top for her cleavage to reveal a lot more. She checked for her phone in her small purse. Ten missed calls, she chuckled to herself. She knew that back home the situation was very nasty. She picked a bottle of beer, her throat tingled a bit as she drank the liquid in huge gulps. At the corner of her eye, she spotted Kevin, the mixed race boy from the local town. He was wearing all white top, jeans and trainers. He had braided hair that revealed a long and handsome face. Katy had tried on different occasions to catch Kevin's attention to no avail. He always played hard to get. Katy could not accept defeat, whatever she wanted she had to get it. She treaded herself carefully amongst the mangle of people dancing everywhere. She kept Kevin in her view because any slight diversion of sight, she would lose him. She walked straight to him and pointed towards the exit. Kevin raised his eyebrow in amazement. The music was too loud that the only way of communication was sign language. Katy persistently pointed outside, Kevin followed her outside reluctantly. The moment they walked outside Katy felt a refreshing wave of wind brushing on her sweat soaked skin. She could feel the coolness on her flushed face. She steadied herself and smiled provocatively at Kevin who remained calm and looked at her bemused .Katy touched Kevin's arm lingeringly "Kevin, I am so glad you are here. I need a massive favour".

Kevin coughed nervously and coercively replied, "Go ahead".

Katy walked towards the car park. She beckoned Kevin to follow her with a finger. They walked slowly towards the car. Katy felt the cold on her bare legs. Her short skirt kept sliding up and she pretended to be bothered by it and pulled it down .She took out the car keys and unlocked the doors using the remote. She glanced stealthily at Kevin and smiled at the anticipated reaction of the car. Kevin stood in his tracks and laughed in disbelief. "You are joking right? Whose baby is this?" Katy pretended she did not hear the question. She opened the door and got into the drivers seat slowly .She put the key in the ignition and said, "Well thanks a lot my dear. That is the massive favour I needed, for you to walk me to my car."

She stroked the steering wheel carefully, "Kevin there is so many times I have tried to talk to you but you just blanked me. I only wanted to hook you up with some people who know how to sell these sweet auto mobiles." She fumbled with the keys at the same time waiting for Kevin to speak. She smiled softly as she noticed that he had run out of words and he stammered, "Well err..."

"Katy" she prompted quickly.

"Yes, Katy of course ... I know you girl. I was just surveying you from a distance" .Kevin walked around the car, touching it smoothly as if it was a precious jewel. He could not believe his fortune. He felt like kicking himself. Why did he not notice that this girl was rich? He smiled to himself as he imagined the wonder full prospects that lay for him if he has to know Katy better.

Kevin was a person who had learnt to live his life independently .He was self sufficient in all terms. When growing up, he suffered from cultural alienation. His father was a white farmer who had settled from Netherlands to Zimbabwe. His mother was a true village woman and she had told Kevin how she met his father on a farm she worked on.

"It was romance at first sight" his mother used to say.

Kevin did not understand though, why his father left Africa for Netherlands .He could hardly remember his father. The last memory he had of him is when he used to take him on the horse when he was five years old and they would ride around the farm, inspecting the harvest and giving remunerations to the workers. As a mixed race young man, when growing up around his friends and at school, he could not identify himself neither as white nor black. Many of his friends used to tease him, "you are half cast. You were originally created as white only in the middle did they decide to make you black".

He had developed a thick skin towards these taunts. He had learnt to fight his way around such people. Things got worse when his mother died and he was adopted by the same uncle who had looked after his mother." Uncle Joe" is what they used to call him . At Uncle Joe's house many cousins lived there, most of them were unruly. Kevin felt protected whenever he walked around with his muscle bulging and smoke addicted cousins. He idolized them so much that he decided to follow their example. He noticed that people were no longer calling "half cast" only "home boy". He really enjoyed his newly acquired status.

As he touched, Katy's car he could not believe his luck and how easy it had been to come across .He cast a glance at Katy and said, "I would love to get to know you"

Chapter 2

The villagers were dancing around an open fire. Drums were beating and clapping hands were matching to the sounds. The air mingled with the sweet aroma of game meat, which was roasting on the open fire .The old men were sitting on the benches drinking their beers and belching. Young men were dancing and stamping their feet, showing off their village toned bodies in an effort to impress the girls. Some girls were giggling shyly at the young men for making such an effort. Other girls including Tracy were dancing back at the men , showing off their skills .Their virgin breasts were visible under the thin-layered tops that they wore. The girls had decorated themselves with beads made from dried round nuts joined together by a string. The earrings were dried sticks that they plucked out of their sweep sticks at home. Their lips were black from the soot they rubbed on.

The dust was rising and giving a natural powdered smell mixed with the salty sweat from the people.

Winnie and the other girls were helping the older women with the preparation of thick porridge *sadza* and making the tomato and onion soup, accompanied by the fat dripping meat on the fire.

For Batsi this was a chance for him to drink lots of traditional strong beer brewed for seven days of alcohol fermentation. He loved these monthly gathering because he always got a chance to chat to one of the village girls. He knew strongly that he was old enough to become a husband. The village's elders never made it easier for him either; they reminded him that he had a responsibility to carry his father's name through out the generation. They rebuked him for drinking heavily and assaulting his siblings.

Deep down Batsi knew that there was every bone of truth in their advice. He knew his weakness was alcohol and that it influenced his behaviour. Only he could not stop.

He craved the salty grains of the alcohol shifting through his mouth. When sober, he felt pity for his siblings , especially Winnie .He knew the amount of responsibility that Winnie took on herself when their parents died. Batsi could vividly remember how much they had suffered ever since their father died from a mysterious illness. Their mother had struggled a lot to raise them single-handed.

The family dealt with a second tragedy when their mother died suddenly within a week of complaining heart problems. Batsi had been in denial for a long time on the death of his parents. He felt cheated of his own life for he knew that he would not enjoy his money and freedom as much. As soon as Winnie got a job as a nurse at the local village clinic, Batsi left his job as a miller and found solace in alcohol and women. His decision did not go down too well with the extended members of the family who felt he was letting his siblings down. Batsi could not face to their criticisms and he would retaliate by being verbally abusive and violent towards such critics. In that mayhem, he would not spare his siblings.

Batsi cavorted after his sister's friend, Tracy. He had seen that she had grown into a well-built woman. He liked the rawness and rudeness o f her character .Batsi knew that he had to make his interest in Tracy known as soon as possible before she had got too serious with the local bully Ben. Batsi was not scared of Ben and he knew that Ben was wary of him.

A local elderly man came to where Batsi was sitting and perched himself right next to him. Batsi sat up startled from his deep thoughts. He recognized the man as Tonga, the local beer maker of the village.

"Excuse me" The man made his intentions to sit down as the custom allowed. "Yebo", Batsi answered back politely and greeted the man. The man exchanged the greetings. Tonga had a face that resembled an owl. He was short man but always made it up by working very hard for his family. Tonga cleared his throat and spat up the phlegm that was blocking his throat. He took his own beer calabash, rinsed his mouth, and spat the beer out.

" It was a challenging day. The sorghum and millet for the beer had to be soaked. I wish I could get young men like you , strong and knowledgeable , to help me in the fields. It would make a difference for me. I am an old man now".

Kevin watched as Tonga took another gulp of the beer and nodding in approval to the masterwork of his hands. After wiping his mouth with the back of his crackly mud caked hands , Tonga placed the beer calabash on the ground . He paused and looked at Batsi waiting for him to answer to his proposal. Batsi rubbed his hands hastily on his thighs and replied, "Well, that is a lovely proposal, but I would prefer drinking the beer than preparing it. What joy do I get from preparing something I will eat?

Tonga chuckled and looked at his beer calabash thoughtfully. "Young man, you are very fortunate for all the things that you have around you. It was different from my day when we had to do work for our food and our beer. Now young boys of this generation boast around showing off what they did not sweat. When I look in this village, I can't help but to feel disgusted at the way you young men have turned this village out."

Batsi looked at Tonga astonished at his choice of words.

"Yes I will repeat again, disgusted!" Tonga banged his fist on the side of the bench, his face scowled. The sides of his mouth were frothy.Batsi made his excuses and left. He did not want to loose his temper with the old man. As he walked towards his sister who was working hard to serve food to the villagers, he noticed Tracy laughing loudly within a group of girls. They were on a break from dancing and drinking water from dried pumpkin shells.

From the group Tracy noticed Batsi looking at him. She winked her left eye at him and laughed out loudly when Batsi looked away. She did not care any less at the irritated way the older women looked at her. She knew fully well that it was disrespectful and morally loose if young women like her giggled loudly as she was doing. She defied all those traditional rules .She felt they were suffocating and irrelevant.

Tracy walked gracefully towards Batsi, swinging her hips from side to side. She stood in front of him and put her hands on her hips. "You pretend you did not see me winking at you Batsi. I know you saw me" She wriggled her finger at Batsi as a mother telling off a naughty child. She did not wait for Batsi to answer her, she continued, "I can see you are hungry. What type of sister do you have? She is busy feeding the villagers and forgetting her own brother?"

"When I hit her people will say I am violent", Batsi said with a pitying tone .He continued "Yes I have been here since the beginning of this gathering and no food .To make matters worst my own sister ...." Batsi raised his voice a bit higher and repeated, "Yes to make it worst, my own sister, my own flesh and blood, she is in the food section. She cannot even spare a plate for her brother. You know what I am going to eat Tracy?" he did not wait for the reply "I am going to eat bones! Meat bones! Nxa"! He clicked his tongue and made a pattern in the sand with his shoe.

Tracy giggled sarcastically and changed her tone to a harsh one "Oh will you be quiet! Just shut up! Did you catch any game? Do you even own a dog used by the special village hunters? My Ben, my boyfriend helped in catching that meat you are crying for. What type of a man are you who cry for something he did not work? Please just stop all this mourning"

Batsi knew that one of Tracy's wild characters was her misuse of language. She had a rotten tongue on her. She was disrespectful and did not care whom she was talking to. Still he liked her for that .He was very drawn to this woman. He could not help but feel his heart beat for Tracy. He had a soft spot for her. H e chuckled nervously, "So you think that Ben catches better game meat than me? "

Tracy replied, waving her hands in the air, "I know for sure. What reputation does he have in the village, is it not for his bravado that people know him for? He is a real man."

Batsi sighed, not out of tiredness, only out of jealous and fury. He disliked the way people viewed Ben. He felt the praises were all for the wrong reasons.Batsi knew that he had to get Tracy to see he had the potential of gaining a reputation in something positive. He looked at Tracy intently and said

"Well last time I checked, he had a reputation for stealing. All this bravado talk you tell me I have not witnessed it .I can assure you though that I witnessed him stealing." Batsi changed his tone and softly continued, "Tracy, I am a real man, its only circumstances that makes me look pitiful like this. I have watched you grow. Do you not remember I used to buy you candy when you were in high school? Alternatively, do you forget too soon? I have not told you this but I completely have feelings for you. If you love me back, I will fetch your water, firewood, catch you the tastiest game meat you could ever have for the rest of your life.Don't insult my ears by mentioning Ben. Does he ever do all the things I plan to do for you? We are hard workers in my family, look at my sister Winnie. She looks after our home, goes to work and still manages to be humble and respectful. Do you think she fell out of the sky? She was born to the same parents who gave birth to me. Can you not see it is in our blood? I can make you happy, just say yes and your life will not be the same ever again" He finished his sentence by taking Tracy's hand in his.

Tracy paused for a moment and said, "For a man you talk too much .Anywhere let me get you a plate of food." She started to walk away and then stopped in her tracks, turned around and faced Batsi then she told him commandingly "Batsi I will accept, you have to know that I am not a one man girl. So do not pin me down with some rules .I am my own woman. Take it or leave it"

Batsi smiled, nodded, and watched as Tracy walked towards the pots that the village women were busy tending.

Winnie took a pinch of salt and dropped it in the tomato and onion soup, she tasted the soup by dipping her index finger onto the wooden spoon which was glimmering in the rich sauce. She frowned as she felt the burning sensation of the smoke from the cooking wood that was getting into her eyes. She wiped her eyes with the corner of her faded top. She gave the soup another stir and stood up for some fresh air as she sniffed back the mucus that was almost dropping off from her nose. She raised her eyes to the sky as she tried to get the most of the air into her eyes.

When her eyes grew accustomed to the dark night, she could see the people sitting down and standing in groups as they took a break from dancing. She looked on the other side of the fire and saw her friend Tracy talking to her brother. She could only wonder what the conversation was all about and did not like the combination at all. She knew if they were discussing anything else apart from general talk, it spelt trouble. She watched as Tracy walked towards her with a huge grin on her face. Winnie smiled back at her friend and welcomed her. She stretched her hands out in an effort to relax her muscles that were aching from the manual labour of lifting the huge earth pots.

"Your dancing was really captivating Tracy", Winnie continued, "All the village boys were looking at you".

Tracy frowned as if to avert her friend's comments, "I know Winnie, that is were my talent lies and you are right. Firstly, I have Ben after me and now it is your brother. It's hard being me", she finished bossily. Winnie felt a sharp pang in the bottom of her stomach. That is what she was dreading the most, her brother and Tracy together. She had her brother to tolerate at home and if Tracy was to get married to, him it would mean more tolerance and she felt she could not have enough patience to continue.

She pretended the news had no effect on her at all and added dryly, "What did you say then?"

Tracy looked at Winnie stunned. "What? Are you foolish? Of course, I said yes. Am I the fortune girl alive or what? What girl in the village have you heard ever receiving such proposals, especially from the top village boys, Batsi and Ben? If you were not my friend, I would have thought you are completely daft. Come on..." she nudged Winnie on the shoulder, "give me a plate of sadza, soup and a big piece of that meat. If you can't look after your brother, I will my dear". She finished off giving Winnie a small punch on the shoulder.

Winnie could feel the power in her legs going. Her legs were almost buckling. She composed herself quickly and knew that she had to act as if she had no problem with the arrangement Tracy had made with her brother. She took a clean empty plate from the floor and wiped it with the corner of her skirt then scooped a huge lump of the thick white porridge that was steaming hot. She added a big spoonful of the simmering soup and proceeded to break the thigh part of the game meat. She knew her brother-liked pepperish food, therefore picked a medium sized stem of chilli and placed on the side of the plate. "Well, hope for the best for both of you", Winnie reluctantly said as she handed the plate to Tracy, and quickly turned to face the opposite direction and joined the other women who were clearing the plates. She bent down and scooped the left over food into a huge dish. She imagined the future .The possibility of her brother and Tracy swearing and getting drunk in front of her siblings. Winnie swallowed hard and realized there was nothing anyone could do to stop the messy situation from happening.

* * *

Gareth slept on the sofa that night. He could not bear going to his bedroom while he knew that his sister was out there joy riding with his brand new car. He thought how inevitable it was for him. He felt useless as he pulled the duvet over his nose. His mother had tried to calm him down and he did feel guilty for not listening to her. Since his father had died years ago, he had made a promise to make child rearing easier for his mother by being obedient. Only when they were all growing up, did he find harder to listen especially when it involved his younger sister, Katy. Gareth felt strongly that their mother spoilt Katy as their father had died when she was young. Their mother constantly reminded them that by seriously rebuking Katy it would make her miss their father more as she was at the disadvantage of not getting to know him properly. The guilt their mother carried was a great contributor to how Katy behaved, Gareth always told his mother.

Gareth made an effort to sleep but could not close his eyes. All he could hear in the living room was the clock ticking .It contributed to his annoyance as he felt every time the clock ticked; it spelt the end of his car. There was a click at the door as keys turned in the lock. The door swung open and Katy staggered in. Gareth jumped up quickly from the sofa, adjusted his jumper and stood in the middle of the living room while folding his arms across the chest. A million reactions were going through his mind. He thought of slapping, shouting, cursing and yelling at his sister. Then he thought of his mother who was sleeping a few rooms away.

Gareth could see Katy from the moonlight reflecting through the lace curtains. He walked over to the lamp on the side table near the TV cabinet, switched it open, and resumed his position still folding his arms across his shoulders. He watched as Katy stood in her tracks, glaring at him. Her face strewn with black mascara and her hair messy, Katy resembled a zombie .There were traces of sticky yellow and white bits on the side of her hair, which resembled vomit. She looked a total mess. At that moment, Gareth was not angry any more. He felt guilty for letting his sister get to the point of making a mockery of herself. He could not even bother to ask for his car. He walked over to where his sister was standing, unsteady on her feet as she tried to balance on her high heels. He snatched his car keys out of her hand .Gareth looked at his sister pitifully and said, "Go and bath" and walked out of the room towards his bedroom.

* * *

The next morning Andrea woke up to peace and silence. She panicked as she remembered how Gareth was the previous night. She hoped nothing fatal had happened and quickly slipped into her dressing gown and slippers. She heard a giggling sound from the kitchen. Andrea let out a sigh of relief as she realized it was her daughter Katy talking on the phone.

When she reached the kitchen, Katy was still on the phone, completely ignoring her mother and continued crunching on her break fast cereals.

If only her daughter had known her father she would be content emotionally, Andrea thought to herself. All the guilt of how her other children had benefited from the love of both parents, unlike her youngest, flooded in her mind. How could she make her youngest child know that she is still as precious and an important member of the family?

Her thoughts trekked back to when Katy had displayed the first signs of rebellion. As a teenager, she would attend parties with her friends, although her son, Gareth, opposed it. To Andrea, it was a way of making up for Katy's loss .Katy's love of parties continued and got worse as she came home late and drunk, still Andrea could not find a way to discipline child. She blinked her tears back as she thought how her husband was the disciplinarian of the family since their kids were born in England. She recalled how he was tough on Gareth to grow up a responsible man. Life was not fair; she thought to herself, it had robbed her of her lovely husband and the children of a doting father.

Andrea felt a tear dropping down one side of her cheek, which she quickly wiped off with the back of her hand. She checked to make sure her daughter had not seen it, in which case Katy was still on the phone and did not notice.

"Katy", Andrea called softly, only to deaf ears as Katy kept talking. "Katy!" shouted Andrea.

"What?" Katy replied with a disappointed look on her face and whispered on the mouthpiece of her phone. "Hold on its only mum".

She turned her attention to her mother and gestured with her hands hurrying her mother to speak.

"Get off the phone", Andrea said, dreading the argument that would ensue soon after Katy had complied. She watched as her daughter rolled her eyes in dismay and brazenly replied ," No!" and continued talking on the phone.

Andrea went over to where Katy sat and grabbed the phone from her hand. Katy pinned down her mother's hand on the table and squeezed hard.Andrea winced in pain and watched as her daughter gritted her teeth, "Mum never do that again".

13

Andrea winced again and she could not bring herself to beg her Daughter to let go. She did not want to make a mistake of appearing weak to Katy. As she thought of what to do next, she heard, Thwarp! She saw Katy bending on the floor holding her cheek in pain and shock. Before Andrea realized it, Gareth was picking Katy from the floor like a little doll and throwing her so hard to the wall that Andrea could hear the impact of breaking bones with the wall. Andrea screamed as she saw her daughter lying on the floor in a heap and seeing her son going in for the kill.

She leapt and struggled to push Gareth away from Katy, "No, no, no, leave her alone, kill me...kill me Gareth." She battled with the weight of her heavy built son for she knew if she did not, Katy would not survive to tell the tale. She buried her head into her son's chest and dug her left leg on the floor firmly to gain more balance.

She kept pushing Gareth away and thought she was going to faint with the energy she was exerting onto her son's body that was not bulging at all. Andrea dropped on the floor when Gareth let go off her. Her body shook as she collapsed in a flood of tears .Looking around her, she saw her daughter groaning and writhing on the floor in pain. Andrea felt her stomach tighten into a knot as she reached for her daughter's phone, which was on the floor and dialled 999 for an ambulance.

* * *

Chapter 3

Kevin dropped his cigarette on the floor and pressed it with his foot. He enjoyed spending the afternoons with his cousins standing at the gate of their house .Uncle Joe hated that habit and he would shout to them to stop making his home resemble a beer hall. The heat from the sun was scorching the ground making it impossible to step on the ground with bare feet. The suburb was busy with noise from people who were selling fruits, vegetables, papers, frozen drinks and dried meat. On the road, people were going around minding their business. Some were women rushing to the market to buy stocks for their kitchens; others were children making their way home from school.

"That's my money man, leave it". His cousins were play-fighting searching each other's pockets. Kevin laughed at his ever-playful mates.

"Grow up" he beckoned lazily.

Blessed, one of his cousins cut in, "What's wrong with you man, Don has my money for cigarettes. You are in a funny mood today. What is it?"

Kevin cast a glance at his cousins and smiled, "I hit the jackpot; I am in a business mood."

Don his other cousin pushed Blessed away and seriously summoned his cousin, "Tell us Kevin, you know when it comes to money ideas we share everything. Business is slow; we have been dry for a few months now. With no money, the old man will force us into secular work. Tell us Kevin"

"Yeah come on, "Blessed echoed.

Kevin paused for a moment and slowly took out a cigarette from his pocket. He was not in a hurry with the information. He stretched out his hand for a box of matches. His cousins quickly scrambled into their pockets in a rush to attend to him. He examined the box that Blessed had handed to him and drew out a stick which he used to light the cigarette. He puffed on it for a while then said, "I hit the jackpot my friends. These hands…,"he outstretched his hands to his cousins who reviewed them as if there was something on them, he continued unperturbed, "This hands are made for money. That is their purpose. Yeah?"

His cousin Blessed shuffled impatiently and said, "You are young at this game Kev, we taught you how to make money the big man way. If you have hit a jackpot, tell us. Not all this hesitancy you are displaying"

Kevin blew out a puff and replied smoothly, "Patience, patience my fellows… haha. You people make me laugh. Anyway I met this babe at a club couple of nights ago .I have always known has something for me for a while now but I kept putting her off because she is vulgar"

His cousins roared out in laughter. They stamped their feet in an exaggerated manner and clapped their hands together.Kevin ignored them and continued smoking his cigarette in a calm fashion.

Don wiped the tears he had in his eyes for laughing hard. He struggled to speak, as he kept on having laughing fits, "You…..hahahahaha… you". He calmed himself and continued, "You, worrying that the girl is vulgar.pot calling kettle black! Since when do you worry about vulgar girls? Kevin please is serious. Anyway, what does this have to do with the business? Leave us alone if you have nothing profitable to tell us."

Kevin continued acting nonchalantly .He threw the small butt of the cigarette on the floor and watched it as it burnt away then said ,"Look at the cigarette on the floor, laugh at me and you will end up like it. Devoured! The girl is vulgar .For your own education, I like being vulgar but I do not like my girls to be the same! They cause all sorts of problems."

"People change, we give you the benefit of the doubt. Why this girl? How does she connect to the business"? Blessed asked his cousin persuasively.

Kevin clapped his hands gratefully," Well done Blessed, You are talking like the man I know." Kevin looked around to make sure there were no prying ears and continued, "This girl is loaded, she drives a brand new ice berg, Mercedes my brothers," he added in a low hushed serious tone. "If I play my cards right we will make serious money".

Don was holding his mouth in disbelief. He cleared his throat and commented," These African sisters are inheriting money from their fathers. Is she a child of a dignitary"?

"No". Kevin answered boastfully. "She is an English girl and she lives in one of these posh places. She is stunning, only her character is zero. Quite young 20 years".

"Woo", Blessed whistled, "That is a jackpot sir! If you play your cards right you are fine .Kevin this does not have anything to do with her behaviour. Business and pleasure do not mix. Invest whilst you are still young. You are at a lovely age .24! I remember when I was your age 20 years ago... I used to live a life of hustling. Make hay while the sun still shines."

Kevin nodded in agreement and felt sorry for his cousins who he grew up admiring only for them to turn up into disappointments. What was left of the once muscle bulging men he grew up idolizing were pitifully thin men who scavenged for information on where to get money through dodgy ways.

His cousins never settled down. They were into paying prostitutes, which Kevin frowned upon. Kevin accompanied his cousins in dodgy deals and sometimes he would take part or stand aside as a witness. The deals ranged from selling fake bank notes to selling basic commodities on the black market. On good days, they earned some money and on bad days, they had nothing. There were several cases when they had a brush with the law, they would serve the community service for their minor offences and carry on. They would though, carry themselves cautiously as Don used to say ", Once bitten, twice shy".

Katy was aching all over her body ,she could feel the pain searing through her left arm that the doctors had told her mother she had broken on impact with the wall. She reflected how she felt scared for her life when her brother was beating her. Her mind was spinning as she felt hatred for her brother. He had placed her in hospital and it was a great inconvenience on her social life. "Mum". Katy whimpered.

"Yes baby". Her mother turned around from the window where she was staring out.

Katy struggled to sit up and her mother came to her aid and assisted her in sitting up straight.

She held her plaster casted arm and touched her mother's arm. She had to make sure her plan worked so she knew her mother was emotionally vulnerable and she could easily manipulate her. "Mum", Katy whispered and put on sad face, "I am not coming home".

Her mother looked at her panicked for her words were a bitter pill to swallow. "Why?"

"Well." Katy continued thoughtfully "Gareth almost killed me mum. You saw how he hit me. I will not go back to live under the same roof as him and I mean it."

She watched as her mother tearfully stared on the floor and said, "I will never allow that to happen. It will be fine. He was angry about the …"

"Nonsense".Katy cut off her mother, "Mum that is rubbish.You are defending him as usual. If dad were here, he would never allow Gareth to hit me like that. You allowed him! I move out or he does, Mum it's your choice". She sulkily turned away from her mother. She felt her mother's soft hands brushing her cheek and she knew her wish was manifesting.

"I will sort it out". Her mother picked up her handbag, "I am getting a cup of coffee from the vending machine, see you in a minute." she walked out of the room and the door closed behind her.

Katy could not contain her happiness. Her plan had worked .Getting Gareth out of the house would ensure she lived her life which ever she liked. To her, her mother was a complete walkover .Gareth was the disciplinarian in the house and he would always nag her to change her ways. She could not stand him.

Katy reached for her phone that was ringing. "Hello" she smiled when she recognized Kevin's voice .He was asking if they could meet up. Katy could not believe her ears. He was calling to meet up! She coyly agreed and smiled to her self as she placed the phone on her bedside cabinet.

She struggled to get out bed. She had to meet Kevin that night even if it meant escaping from the hospital .Her plan was to get money from her mother and call one of her friends to bring clothes for her. She limped towards the toilet, sat on the bowl to relieve her, and limped back to her bed to bask in her happiness.

Gareth walked to the hospital entrance. He quivered with anxiety of meeting up with his mother. He knew it would be hard for his mother to forgive him. Staring at the flowers he bought for his sister, he worked out how the meeting will turn out .Apologising was the last thing on his mind. He was furious when he saw his sister pinning their mother on the table. Katy had gone too far and this was the first step to abusing his mother, Gareth had angrily thought .He could not remember the attack on his sister because adrenaline blinded his mind. The intention of the hospital visit hospital was to comfort his mother. He had enough of his sister. It was time he had called for a family meeting to resolve the threat to family unity.

Gareth went through the automatic doors towards the reception. He instantly recognized his mother in the small café at the side of the reception sipping on coffee. He smiled broadly and walked over to her. As he learnt over to kiss her, she turned around and her face was wretched in fury. "What are you doing here?" she asked at the same time pushing him away from kissing her. "Have you come to kill her or see if she is dead?"

Gareth stared at his mother, aghast. "For goodness sake mum! She is my sister why would I kill her?"

His mother frowned, "What do you call the atrocity you committed yesterday? Sisterly love?"

Gareth pulled out the chair next to his mother and placed the daffodils on the table. He intently fixed his eyes on his mother, rubbed his eyes and let out a big sigh. His mother kept looking forward. That is the first time Gareth had seen his mother looking her age. Her wrinkles had appeared on her face and she appeared rugged.

Gareth was short of words at first as his mind wrestled .He sighed again and leant forward, "Mum, I will never apologise for beating the hell out of Katy. She is too spoilt .Did you not realize what she did to you. Is it better for her to beat you than for me her brother to discipline her".

His mother's eyes were blazing with anger as she faced him, "So the best way is to break her arm? Right? I cannot believe we are having this conversation! You almost killed your sister .The best you can say is you won't apologise?"

Gareth calmly replied, "Mum if I apologise to Katy, she will think that all she does is right, she has no limits, it is not too late to instil some manners into her .She does not respect you and you just let her get away with it, you....."

"Don't you ever dare criticize my parental ways again. If I am not that fit do you think you sprung from the ground like a mushroom and just bloomed?" His mum curtly remarked.

Unable to argue with his mother Gareth stood up and said, "Mum please pass these flowers to Katy and I will se you at home"

"No."

"Mum are you sleeping here then?"

"No, you are not sleeping in the house and pack your things," His mum could not even bear to look at him as she delivered the hurtful words.

Gareth thought his mother was being too emotional so he sat back on the chair and shook his head in disbelief ", Mum, what are you insenuating? I know that emotions are flying all over but please don't say things we will all regret".

"You heard me, I want you out of the house before you murder any of us. Either your age mates are married or living on their own. What of you Gary? Still living at home and beating your baby sister".

Gareth felt every word sink in his ears hurting like someone was dropping hot wax. He placed his hand on top of his mother's and softly and said, "Are you sure of what you are saying mum?"

His mother nodded and took her hand from him. She continued with no emotion showing on her face, "And stay away for some time until the dust settles down. When we are ready, I will let you know".

Gareth protested, "Mum...that is a bit extreme don't you think? You want to cut me out of your life .I will give you a week and when you are calm we can sit down as a family and tal....."

His mother raised her hand in the air interrupting him. She nodded her head and said, "Take care, Gareth. I will call you in my time. Surely after what you did that is the best you can do to give us time?"

Gareth stood up angrily and pushed the chair to the other side. He swept the flowers from the table and banged the table in a manner that some of the coffee splashed on his mother, who moved back to avoid being burnt. He did not care about the audience who were gathering to watch what was going on. He walked away and did not look back at his mother.

Chapter 4

Ben frantically looked for his axe. He was pacing aimlessly in the compound and cursing under his breath. At the same time shaking his mother's hands off his legs. He was literally dragging his mother who was begging him not to take the weapon.

He kept pleading angrily with his mother, "Mother, please let me be. I need to show that boy .Leave

Me". He tried to untangle his mother's hands from his leg but they were stuck as if they had super glue.

Ben clicked his tongue, "Nxa! Mother! How many times do I have to plead with you? Please leave me. You are just a woman. This is a man's issue. Please understand. Look you are getting bruised".

His mother kept holding on like a tick on a cow's hide. Ben stopped fighting off his mother .She was too old for dragging around the compound like a rug. He continued protesting, "Mother leave me, I am not doing anything anymore."

Still, that would not stop his mother from lurching on .Ben relaxed his body and held his mothers hands. She seemed to relax too and she looked at him in a pleading way .Ben walked away and headed towards the back of the mud kitchen hut. He picked gritty sand and rubbed it on his hands until they looked red raw in pain. He let out a whimper and bent down holding his hands in his hands. He could not believe the rumour he had heard at the cattle dipping station.

Batsi was having an affair with his woman Tracy. He felt emasculated. How dare he step in his territory? Who did he think he was? To Ben, it was Batsi challenging him to a fight. He was prepared to fight him like a man. Although, he thought, it was better to chop him up. He could not bear his reputation go down the drain because of a common boy!

Ben was determined to revenge. He did not want Batsi to humiliate him. They had never been matched in the warriors fight so he did not know how strong Batsi was. Ben himself was a strong built man and was very dark in complexion that in the dark if he did not smile people would blend him with it. He always walked in a pompous way. He was not very good looking, with a fat flat nose and big eyes he could easily resemble a bull. He used the size of his body to intimidate people and get his way.

As he planned revenge, he knew he had to hurt something that Batsi was proud of in his life. He nodded satisfactorily as he realized exactly how he was going to hurt Batsi.

* * *

After work, Winnie preferred to rush straight home so she could be on time to welcome her younger siblings home from school. That was the only way she could shake Tracy off because at work Tracy stalked Winnie. She would abandon her nursing post so she would brag to Winnie how wonderful her brother was at certain aspects of the bedroom life that Winnie always found revolting.

Winnie was a strong believer of sexual relations after marriage. She was very proud she was a virgin and she treasured it so much that it had contributed to her not having a boyfriend at her age. She always imagined herself married to a man who would take care of her and consider her needs and feelings. Tracy teased her on that issue, sometimes calling her "madam virgin". Hence Winnie

Was glad she could have some time to meditate as she walked home from work.

That afternoon the sun was blazing and little bush fires were starting across the dry veld. They did not spread because the ground was mostly sand than grass. Winnie enjoyed walking across the plain fields. There were no houses nearby. It was peaceful and all she could hear were cows mooing from a distance, a distant shout of the herd boys herding them. She walked slowly, carelessly, and deep in thought,

"Boo!"

Winnie jumped and was startled to see the owner of the voice, Ben. She completely disliked him and he knew that.

"Princess Winnie".

Winnie looked at Ben anxiously and stammered ", y... ye...yes".

"Princess Winnie the one that people adore, the one who is so pure. The one that your brother Batsi boasts off in the whole village as untouched and clean". He finished sarcastically.

Winnie checked her surroundings in the hope a person would stray and she shrugged nervously as the only people around were her and Ben. In her mind, she was looking for a way to escape. The veld was too wide and the only way it would lead to was the forest, whether she was running back to the hospital or home. She also knew she did not stand any chance with Ben, one of the best athletes of the village.

Ben seemed to read her mind when he said, "No, if I were you I would not even hurt my brain by thinking the unthinkable. It's just you and me Winnie."

Winnie winced in disgust as she thought of what Ben was planning to do to her, she started, "Take the money Ben and leave me alone .Is that what you want? Take all of it. Please let me be on my way. She tried to move forward but Ben was deliberately blocking her way and finding the whole situation amusing. He whistled and said, "Never will I let you go. You are my golden ticket Winnie.You are the only one I can use to show your brother who rules the kingdom. Would it not be reckless on my part to let you go? That is a bit foolish is it not?" He grabbed Winnie's hand, who began struggling.

Winnie could feel her heart beating in her mouth. She thought she was going to pass out. Well, it was better than witnessing what Ben was thinking of doing to her. She dug her teeth into his arm. He slapped her on her cheek. The pain sent waves across her whole face.

Still she knew she had to stop him dragging her to an isolated short bushy tree that he was dragging her to. She felt like a cow going for slaughter as he pinned her on the floor. The dust and dirt on the ground went into her mouth.

Her ribs crushed under the weight of Ben who was tossing her like a piece of meat. She struggled and kept lying on her stomach but did not stand any chance, as Ben was far stronger than she was. He yanked her on her back, roughly pulling up her skirt. His face had changed into an evil and demented one.

Winnie tried to push him off but the more she did the weaker she got. Still, she did not want to give up. She kept wriggling around in an effort to prevent Ben from accomplishing his evil deeds. She felt her underwear cutting her skin as Ben tore if apart. She screamed when Ben pushed her legs apart, making her muscles sore. She tried to scream again but Ben held her mouth and she could not let any sound out. Tears were streaming on the side of her cheeks. Winnie could not breathe with the tearing pain that followed as Ben forced himself onto her. She could see her mother's face and her siblings, and then she went blank.

* * *

Winnie slowly opened her eyes and all she could see was pitch darkness. She tried to gather her mind to recollect where she was. Was she in her room? If yes, why was it thorny on the floor? She slowly raised her body from the ground and fell back in pain. That is when it hit her. The last thing she remembered was the pain. It was too intense. She squeezed her eyes shut in fear that Ben might be nearby, coming back to rape her for the second time.

Winnie slowly gathered herself, counted to three, and heaved herself up. She cried out in pain as all her body parts were tender and sore. It was too dark to see but she was accustomed to the road. She walked slowly and each step was as painful as the whole experience. The journey home seemed to last forever. She could see from a distance the light from the lamp in their kitchen. All Winnie wanted was to go to her hut and lock herself in there. She felt dirty, cheap and worthless .She fumbled with the door and opened it wide. Her young sister and brother were sleeping in her room .They did that when Winnie was late in returning home, which was rare?

Winnie dropped her bag on the floor and collapsed into a corner and started sobbing .Her siblings were deep in sleep and did not wake up to the noise. How could that happen to her, Why her, why? Is all that Winnie could think?

* * *

Katy pushed her dark thick hair back. She had no trouble in convincing her mother to give her 50 dollars .After all she wanted to buy fruits and magazines because hospitals were boring. Her mother had quickly forked out the money quickly out of her purse .She had bade farewell to Katy and told her she would be back the next morning .It was easy escaping the hospital for there were no members of staff around.

Katy limped in the direction of the movie house in First Street .People were looking at her sympathetically and some were even offering to call a taxi for her. She kept shaking her head and saying 'no thanks'. She was almost there. She saw a crowd of people gathered outside the movie house and it was easy to spot Kevin with his light complexion. He smiled weirdly at her specifically focusing on her plastered cast.

Kevin lowered his gaze to meet her eyes and cooed as if he was speaking to a baby, "Are you ok, did you fall?"

"Oh get off, like you are concerned, just a silly accident that I am sure the doctor can fix."

"Yes and you are in the wrong place, are you not supposed to be resting?" Kevin was slightly concerned for her.

Katy frowned, "Whatever! Where are the cousins you were talking about?" Katy laughed when she saw two grown men the age of his uncles in England pop behind Ben. She did not expect it. She stopped laughing when she saw Kevin's bemused look.

"Are you serious? We are going to watch a movie with them?" Katy could not believe it. That would definitely lower her standards. What if she bumped into her friends? What would they think? They would probably wonder if they were being chaperoned.

Kevin seemed to read her mind and he coolly said ", we will go and eat." In addition, he led the way towards the eating-place.

"Hold on ", Blessed interrupted, turning to Katy, he continued, "Why are we walking? Where is your car Katy?"

Katy was a bit puzzled at the interest Blessed showed in her car. "At home .Were you never told that it's illegal to drive with a plaster?" .She walked past Blessed and joined Kevin who was walking in the front.

Kevin offered his arm for support, she smiled at him, and obliged. The eatery was buzzing with many people who were buying food. Most of them were young people who were enjoying a night out. Katy and company had to join the back of the queue. Kevin made his excuses and pulled his cousins aside. Katy could not make out what they were saying but from the queue were they had left her standing she could tell that it was not a calm conversation.

Kevin was pointing at his cousin aggressively, Katy was wondering if he was trying to impose a point on them with the way he was gesturing. His cousins seemed annoyed and angry with him .They were waving their hands in the air .At one moment Katy swore that the three of them stopped their conversation, looked in her direction and continued! It was all too dramatic. Katy reached in her pocket and pulled out a cigarette. She put it between her lips, as she reached for her lighter in her purse, a strong hand grabbed the cigarette from her mouth. She turned around, shocked and her eyes met with Kevin.

"What are you doing?" Katy quizzed.

"Saving your life", Kevin placed the cigarette between his lips.

Katy looked around and she could not see Kevin's cousins .She carelessly announced. "I can see you got rid of those old cousins of yours."

Kevin moved forward, pressed his forehead on hers. She could smell the musky smell of cigarette mixed with man's perfume. Her body tingled with sensation and she closed

Yvonne Ebhodaghe

her eyes .Kevin stroked her cheek roughly and whispered in a rough tone, "Don't disrespect my bruvs".

Kevin moved away from her .Katy opened her eyes and rubbed her arm on Kevin's .She lowered her gaze, and murmured "; I like it when my men are rough".

Her impatience was growing because Kevin had not made any romantic advances. Katy could not make out what type of man Kevin was. He was not a man of morals from what she could judge from his appearances.

Kevin did not react when she brushed her arm on his. The only thing he said was, "If you are really hungry, then we need to go to another place, this one is packed".

Katy got annoyed with the formalities between Kevin and her. She stopped in her tracks, " What's up with all this stuff. You and I know that we want fun. Why are you treating me like a girlfriend on a first date?" she had her hands on her waist.

Kevin drew on his cigarette, puffed up a ring of smoke, seemed to admire it disappearing into the air, and laughed, "Are we not on our first date then? Moreover, I thought you wanted to be my girlfriend".

"Well err…" Katy did not expect that sort of reply. She had never come across a man who talked in a respectful way to her. All men wanted something from her. Kevin was different.

"You are hardly a gentle man… so why are you pretending," she asked anxiously.

Kevin shrugged, "You are right. I am not a gentleman, but I do have my morals."

Katy laughed sarcastically, "Morals? Then I am clean and pure."

"Are you not?" Kevin quizzed.

Katy was confused. She paused and said, "What sort of mind games are you playing? Of course you know I am not a good girl." She made a gesture of inverted commas and continued, "Just tell me what you want. Lets not waste time. We are adults."

"Are we?" Kevin replied coolly and stubbed his cigarette on the floor. He started walking "Are you coming or what?"

Katy dragged her feet and walked in a daze. She could not let him treat her like that. She never allowed anyone to make her feel weak. She stopped again and angrily demanded for Kevin to explain himself. In turn, he seemed rather annoyed with her and just continued walking. That alone send her blood boiling .She grabbed his arm roughly and slowly said, "You did not answer my question, what game are you paying here? Tell me.

Kevin turned around when Katy grabbed his arm. He could not believe the cheek of her. She was a persistent woman. He relaxed the arm that Katy was holding and sighed deeply. What was happening to him? The reason he had argued with his cousins was that they were encouraging him to execute their plan of stealing the car away from Katy.

"Kevin you will drive this girl and we will be waiting at that woodland". His cousin Blessed had suggested excitedly. "When you get there, pretend to park and walk outside to relieve yourself. That is when we the gangsters will jump out of nowhere drag the girl, threaten her a little bit and drive off with the car. We will wear masks so we are unrecognizable. If you follow these instructions we will be rich!"

"No", Kevin had said, "I have changed my mind guys. No we are not doing this.I think I like this girl. And I am not sure I would like to fleece her."

His cousins had rebuked him for being a soft boy. Where were the brave and streetwise antics they had instilled in him? They had questioned. They truly looked disappointed in him. Kevin had felt so bad when they walked away. He knew it would take a lot to persuade his cousins back.

In essence, Kevin was tired with the hustling life. Before she died, his mother had taught him to work hard.

"The food of the hard worker is tasty and fulfilling. The food of the lazy one is bitter and unfulfilling". That one aspect had changed his mind from the whole car jacking idea. He wanted to change his life and he truly liked Katy. To him that rebellion and I do not care attitude was just a front. He could see himself in Katy. Not wanting to blend with other people, refusing to show weaknesses. Kevin though could see the potential in Katie .To him, she was a girl who lacked direction and responsibilities. He could not bear to hurt her especially in the state she was. He knew the broken arm was a result of an ugly situation that had culminated.

He held out his other hand to Katy and slowly removed her gripping off his arm. They began walking hand in hand .The temperatures were dropping and the air was getting nippy. Kevin took off his jacket and placed it over Katy's shoulders, he covered her bare arms .He could see tears in Katy's eyes. He wrapped his arms around her and comforted her as she sobbed on his chest. To Kevin it was a beginning of a new life for him and Katy.

Evil knows no bounds. When his cousins left them, they were seething in anger. They felt Kevin had chosen Katy over them. All their hope of making money had dashed because their cousin had backtracked. Their turmoil was the fact they had helped raise Kevin from boyhood to manhood. What eked them the most was Kevin had lost respect for them. He was no longer listening to them, sometimes sabotaging deals in order to stay out of them. They could not let him carry on with this rebellion. To make matters worst, he had "shown them up" in Katy's presence by arguing with them! When they reached home, they had discussed many delirious plans to revenge their "disloyal cousin who had broken the protocol of "forever brothers". Only time, would tell when they would put their plan into action.

Chapter 5

Batsi was antagonized. He could not believe what his sister had confessed to him. His sister, Winnie, had refused to come out of her room the whole day. He had to break open the door and literally drag her out into the c compound. He had stipulated on her to tell him what the problem was. If not, the only alternative was to pack her things and leave the homestead. He did not expect the answer to be "Ben raped me".

His agony did not lie with his sister's rape. It was Ben. He had impaired the deepest part of his alpha pride. He had violated his sister's purity hence tarnished the family's name forever! Batsi could visual attending the beer festivals and all men sneering and commenting on the blemish dented on the family. Their family had a good standing in the village because of his sisters' commendable behavior.Batsi had managed to acquire favours in nearby villages due to his sister. They would serve him free beer so their male children would in future ask to marry Winnie. As the only man in the family, he stood to acquire a lot of wealth from the bride price. He had prepared to charge the highest bride price to future suitors for his sister was a virgin. Only now, all these hopes and dreams had vanished.

Batsi pulled his sister's hair carelessly .He was exacerbating the situation. "Sit up my friend, stop all this lying. Is that a little ploy that you and Ben devised, that Batsi lose his right to a better bride price? Stop lying I say! Tell the truth."

Winnie cried pitifully, and continued whimpering as her brother pulled her hair painfully. She stammered amidst tears, "I ...i...i... am telling the truth brother Batsi....I ...I... tried to fight him... off... he over... powered me... an....."

"Shut up!" Batsi clapped his hand across his sister's cheek. "You over powered him? So why are you in this situation? Come on stand up ,We will go to Matondo ,the village medicine man ,he will examine you to check if you still the virgin I remember or the prostitute you are now ".He picked his sister from the ground like a rag doll. By this time, a crowd of villagers had gathered outside the compound to witness the latest of Batsi's charade. They knew him for being violent to his siblings. Usually the people who intervened to stop it were the village elders and only if they were summoned .The abuse had reached the point that people were tired of calling the elders, they always hoped he would not cause fatal injuries to his siblings.

Batsi continued dragging his sister across the village as she struggled to keep up.Winnie was begging him to stop embarrassing her in front of the whole village. Batsi thought he had to prove that he was not weak man. Other brave women were clapping their hands and lamenting for Batsi to leave his sister.Batsi would threaten to hit them, they would back off and continue lamenting.

He headed to the medicine men's house with some of the villager's in tow.Batsi dropped his sister on the door and shouted his greetings in a hasty manner to the medicine man. He explained what his mission was. The medicine man beckoned him and his sister inside. He pushed and forced a struggling Winnie inside the hut and closed the door behind him. He stared furiously at the villagers who were clearly disapproving of his actions. He ignored them and waited .It seemed to take a long time , a while later a sobbing Winnie was pushed out of the house by the scrawny ,scruffy looking medicine man who informed Batsi "as useless as an open jar".

Batsi's blood was boiling at that point. He pulled his sister from the ground and headed towards Ben's house. The other villagers were following closely and trying to comfort Winnie who was singing a sad song, she was tired of crying. When they got to Ben's compound, there was no one in sight, Batsi turned to Winnie and sharply said, "If I ever see your face at my house you will regret the day our mother gave birth to you. Stay here. Stay here with your husband!" then pushed Winnie who was tagging on his trousers and begging him not to leave her. He raised his hand in the air threatening to beat her. Winnie responded by backing away and lying on the dirt that covered the ground. Batsi gave the compound one last glance to confirm there was no one in the compound, satisfied he walked away, shoved the spectators to one side and walked away without looking back at his helpless sister.

"Ben, Ben! Come out now....good for nothing boy". Tracy yelled on top of her voice, pacing Ben's compound. She had received the news of Winnie's eloping to Ben's house. Humiliation was an understatement of how she felt. She felt betrayed by her friend and she did not want to believe the rape story. To her, an affair was going on behind her back.

Still yelling she continued, "While you are at it, come out with the wife, Hurry up".

Ben's mother came out and softly asked, "Tracy what is wrong? Is it not too early in the morning to shout? Please, calm down".

"Hush, you old woman, is that what you do? Encouraging your child to get another woman while I am waiting for him to exercise the traditional rites of marriage to my family?"

Ben walked out of his hut and yawned .He pulled up his trousers and lazily said, "Don't talk to my mother like that Tracy. What is wrong with you? Why are you yelling? You want to wake the whole village up?"

Tracy pranced her feet on the ground and let out a huge sarcastic laugh ", heee! You worry about waking the whole village. When news of your eloping is across different villages? What do you take me for? A fool?" She picked up a handful of sand and threw it in Ben's eyes who responded by rubbing it out of his eyes furiously.

"Are you mad? Do you want to blind me?"

"Yes, so those cavorting eyes will stop working! Why my friend though? Moreover, where is she? Bring her out. Useless girl", she clicked her tongue in dismay and spat on the ground. Immediately Winnie walked out slowly out of the kitchen hut .Her eyes were puffed up and were red like pepper. She was still wearing the dress she came with. Her dress torn on the bottom half, and covered in brown dirt mixed with blood spots .She looked a shadow of her usual self. Even Tracy appeared astounded by the state of her friend. Nevertheless, she let pride get the better of her.

She walked over to Winnie and spat in her face ", prostitute... I knew it .You are not as pure as you always proclaimed. Madam virgin! All the discouragement to leave Ben and all along you were planning to take him!"

Ben pulled Tracy from Winnie, which catalyzed her anger more, "Do not touch me, so you are protecting your wife. Yes?"

"Why do you pretend you care? You are having an affair with her brother! Why are you preaching morals?"

"Is that it? I take him, you take her. Is that it?" she stared at Ben ,eyes blazing and continued "if that is the case ,stay together you deserve each other!" .She turned around to Winnie and sneered, "As for you my friend , run when you see my footprints. I will teach you a lesson", she charged out of the compound shouting on top of her voice.

Winnie huddled near Ben's mother .Ben chuckled and ruefully exclaimed, "Tonight you share my room, I saved your life, did I not? She would have killed you". He walked arrogantly to his hut.

Ben's mother hugged a shivering Winnie protectively and led her to the hut.

It was a couple of weeks now that Gareth had not received a phone call from his mother. He had found a spacious and comfortable one bed roomed flat near his work place in the city centre. Everyday was a mountain to climb especially when his phone did not ring.

He felt sorry for his mother and hoped that she was fine. He did not bother to think of his sister for she was the cause of the family scattering. He was missing all the home comforts and his favourite dinners that his mother cooked for him. His mother used to spoil him with roasted potatoes, braised beef, steamed carrots and parsnips and lots of gravy that made his plate all gooey. He kissed his teeth and dropped the Chinese take away box he was holding in his hand. His life was getting worst. Everyday he had to restrain himself from making the first call, for his mother's words kept echoing in his ears, "I will call you in my time". He dreaded how long that time would take .What hurt him the most was his mother's fear that he was a murderer. Anger management issues, yes, but surely not a killer, he wondered to himself.

He had made every effort to make his pad homely. He had a sound knowledge of interior 'deco' and he had bought some wallpaper to make the rooms a bit trendy. He did not have much furniture, just one couch and a TV on its stand. In his kitchen, he had one pot, 1 plate and a spoon and in the bedroom, he had a double bed and a makeshift wardrobe to hang his clothes. How he wished his mother was around to iron and clean for him. "I guess its time I was pushed of the nest," he muttered to himself under his breath as he checked his phone for any messages or missed calls.

* * *

Andrea woke up to midnight darkness. Her heart was pounding in her ears. Her body soaked in her sweat .For a moment she could not place where she was. She was relieved when she saw she was in the comfort of her bedroom .She had a nasty dream. Her mind had been unsettled from the day she drove her son out of the house .She knew out of all her children , Gareth was the most caring . That is why she was shocked at his aggressive behaviour towards Katy.

She almost jumped out of her skin when the phone rang.

"Hello?" she answered through the mouthpiece holding the phone tightly.

"Mum are you ok? Sorry I woke you up .Time differences here, its 10 you know I guess its 12 there?" replied the voice on the other end of the line.

Andrea caressed the phone wire upon hearing the voice of her beloved daughter Fran, based in England.

"I am ok my baby. Its all right I was awake anywhere."

"At this time of the hour.mom are u having a sleep disorder?"

Andrea smiled at the thought of her daughter who often gave diagnosis for any small symptom. Andrea licked her dry lips and said, "Not at all honey. I was just finishing reading my novel". Andrea winced at the thought of lying to her daughter. She did not want to worry her.

There was a second pause and Fran continued, "Very well ma how is Gareth and Katy?"

Andrea felt weak with sorrow .She sighed deeply and said, "Err... they are fine. Katy has been thinking of painting her bedroom ..."

"Ma, I know."

Those words sent Andrea's head spinning, "know what Fran" she pretended.

"I am not a kid anymore ma. Gareth told me everything the day it happened .I have been waiting to see if anything improves but nothing. Not even a phone call to your son".

"Don't be judgemental Fran. Do you know the whole issue? Did he tell you that he almost killed Katy?"

"Mum that is an exaggeration. He did not almost kill her! He obviously let his anger get the better of him. That is not the reason to send him packing".

Andrea irritably replied, "Fran, I was there. He threw Katy to... to the wall. I always have nightmares of what might have happened. I feel I made the right decision. I do not trust leaving Gareth with Katy alone. It was better he moved out. Katy is still young, she needs me."

"Mum!" Fran shouted down the line. "It's high time you discover that Katy is no longer a baby! Since she was a little girl, you had a soft spot for her, guess what? It is not helping! Was she not hurting you, when Gareth intervened ? He could not stand by and watch all that. Katy needs chastising. Besides she is beyond discipline anyway."

Andrea sipped on a glass of water and said, "Fran I am the one with your brother and sister. It is high time that both you and Gareth know I am your mother and respect me! Not dictating to me how to run this family."

"The irony", Fran exclaimed, "it should be Katy you tell that too! We listen to you, does Katy?"

Andrea felt it was a trick question. She explained to her daughter that she had not spoilt Katy. Katy was disadvantaged to grow up with a single parent.

An annoyed Fran quipped, "For goodness sake mum, at that rate no wonder Katy is the black sheep of the family. How many children are from single parent families but they still go ahead and succeed? Why is Katy's case so exceptional? Ma, its time you sort that little girl before she is the end of you."

With that, Fran made her excuses she had to get off the phone and apologised again for waking her mother up.

Andrea replaced the receiver and slumped back on to the bed. She closed her eyes and all she could hear in the silent dark were her ears ringing, in confusion.

Katy ran her fingers through her long blonde hair. She reached for her mirror, adjusted her hair in it and applied lipstick. She had received a message from Kevin asking her to meet up with him at a beauty spot .He had specifically mentioned for her to bring her car. Katy owned a VW golf car. She was so excited at meeting up with Kevin. It had been a while since they had been together. Kevin preferred to communicate by phone. Therefore, Katy had been glad when Kevin had called up.

She started driving towards the town where the beauty spot was. When she got there, there was no one in sight. The gardens were bursting with daffodils and buttercups. The grass was green, well-manicured .The trees were divine, and the surroundings resembled paradise. Katy beamed at the thought of spending a lovely afternoon with Kevin.

She thought of having a sneaky cigarette before Kevin arrived. She stepped out of the car. Immediately she saw two masked men heading towards her. Katy shrieked and started running towards the car. Unfortunately, for her, she was wearing high heels and the men outran her. They grabbed her arm and pushed her to the ground. They took her keys and sped off with her car, leaving Katy howling and throwing herself to the ground.

She was at this unfamiliar place, with no money and no phone. She took off her high heels and ran towards the highway. Cars were speeding by fast. She tried to wave the cars down but to no avail. She broke down again in tears as she watched the cars pass by helplessly. She saw a bicycle that was coming towards her slowly. She started waving it down. It seemed like a long time, fortunately the man on the bicycle stopped. He looked at her strangely and asked what the matter was. Katy fretfully narrated her story to him. The man seemed to feel sorry for her .He offered to lend her his phone to call anyone who could help her. The only numbers that she knew by heart where her mother's and Gareth. She called her mother's mobile phone and there was no reply. She tried the home number and there was no reply .She did not know Kevin's number by heart, where was he?

The man who had lent his phone seemed impatient for he kept glancing at his wristwatch. Katy was getting desperate .She tried her mother's phone for the last time, still no reply. She had no other option but to call her brother. She explained the situation to him and her location. Gareth confirmed he would come to pick her up after half an hour. Katy thanked the man, stood on the grass verge of the highway, and waited for Gareth. She did not want to call him, only now because she was desperate and he was the only one available. She hesitated how the meeting will be, especially after the fighting incident.

Exactly half an hour later, Gareth's silver Mercedes pulled on the hard shoulder of the motorway. Katy got into the car and forced a smile at him. Gareth was wearing dark sunglasses so there was no eye contact between the two of them. Gareth smiled back, and started driving. The whole journey was uncomfortable and both of them were silent. There was soft jazz music playing on the car radio. Katy stole a side way glance and could tell from the unshaven chin that he was homesick. In a strange way she missed her brother at home only she could not allow him to come back to ruin her freedom by giving curfews, locking her in if she ignored them.

She was relieved when the car pulled outside the gate. Katy mumbled a thank you. Her brother still wearing glasses asked, "How is mum?"

"Fine", Katy grumbled.

"Is everything okay at home?"

"Yes".

"Katy I am serious if you so much as hurt mum again I will do worst than last time" .Gareth had changed his tone of voice to a more serious one. Katy did not want to spark the situation off again, so she simply replied, "All is fine, thanks for the ride".

She got out of the car and slammed the door. She could feel her brother's stare right on her back. Katy unlocked the gate and went inside the house. She peered through the curtain and saw her brother's car still parked outside the gate. After a few minutes, the car drove off.

Katy rushed to her bedroom and checked through her diary were she kept all her contacts details. She quickly dialled Kevin's number and asked him why he did not turn up .To Katy's amazement; Kevin denied asking them to meet up. He had been home the whole day. Katy was trembling with disbelief at the way the situation was going. So if it was not Kevin who was it? Moreover, why did the people use Kevin's phone to text her? She told Kevin about the robbery and who sounded shocked at the whole experience. In panic, Katy told Kevin she would call the police. Kevin urged her not to and told her he will sort it out.

Katy began trembling in fear that Kevin might have been behind the whole car jacking, and he was probably pretending to be concerned in order to save his own skin. She quivered at the thought of falling in love with a crook .She instantly felt her body getting a bit cold .As she lay under the duvets, her mind spun around like a twister

Chapter 6

Winnie had endured nights of abuse from Ben. Her body was full of scratches and her small bump was beginning to show revealing her pregnancy. She had managed to meet her siblings on a daily basis on their school route.She was relieved that Batsi had been spending some time away from home ,perhaps spending time with Tracy . She could not go to work because Tracy made her life a misery by threatening her. The breaking point is when people had to hold Tracy back from stabbing her with a syringe. The ward sister thought it was suitable for Winnie to stay home and they would only pay her three months salary. Only earth knew how she would survive from then on.

Ben did not know about the salary and Winnie thought it best to keep it that way. She helped in caring for his mother because she had shown her daughter's love.Winnie detastated the days Ben slept at home. She wished he could stay away most nights as he used to.Winnie had not seen her brother and did not plan too.

That particular morning, Winnie woke up as usual and did her daily chores of cooking and cleaning the homestead .She took the jerry cans and walked towards the water well to fetch some water. She sang softly .Her mind was far. She heard a distant calling of her name and the voice was getting louder and nearer.

"Winnie!"

Winnie turned around and dropped her cans in surprise. The voice belonged to one of her close friends who had been fortunate to live with her sister in the city.

"Portia!" Winnie threw her arms around her friend. Finally, Winnie let go and she had tears rolling down her eyes.

Portia wiped them with her fingers, "I went to your house and saw your brother Batsi. I did not know Tracy was his girlfriend. How do you cope?" Portia laughed lightly,

"Anyway, they were quite rude when I asked after you and they said you are at your husband's house. Nevertheless, Winnie! Ben of all people? My mother keeps me updated with all the village gossip. Ben has worst of recent. Why him though? What happened to the good girl? Turned bad hey?" Portia cajoled her friend.

Winnie sat on the ground and sighed deeply, "Wow Portia my dear, mine is a long story. Sit on the can. I am not in a rush .Let me tell you." She positioned the can for her friend to sit on. The girls sat opposite each other and cried as Winnie related her whole story to Portia.

Afterwards Portia wiped off her tears and said, "This is wrong .What did the village elders do? Why could they not let him stand a village trial? This would not happen in the city. He would be serving time in jail as we are talking now"

Winnie plucked out a stock of green grass and chewed on the sharp edges, precautious of cuts .She laughed, "Portia this is not the city. I just have to suffer and get on with it".

"No, that is why you are coming with me to the city."

Winnie stopped chewing and looked at her friend carefully, "Are you serious?"

Portia smiled unassumingly ", of course Winnie, that way you can rebuilt your life. I now have my own place to stay and I hold a secretarial job at an accounting firm. Please don't say no". Winnie touched her baby bump worryingly and Portia noticed ", don't worry, your baby will be well looked after, I will help you get a job and they are lots of nannies around".

Winnie knew it was an opportunity she could not miss. Her prayers were surely answered. Her main worry though was her siblings. She could not leave the village knowing that Batsi was the main carer.

Winnie thanked her friend, "thank you very much Portia. I would be a fool to say no. My only reason for staying in the village is my siblings. They will suffer or even die of hunger if I leave them with my brother".

"Well", Portia said thoughtfully, "my aunt lives five villages away. The *Huyu* village. It is a long way from here. She is lonely and at her age, it would be practical for her to have some help. I am sure she will not mind looking after Tommy and Chipo. Chipo is 14 isn't it?" Winnie nodded, Portia continued ", and Tommy is 10? As soon as they finish school, you will be able to afford for them to stay with you in the city. In the meantime, you will send money to my aunt.Batsi will never know where they are".

Winnie smiled in relief at knowing that her siblings would be fine. The two young women hatched an escape plan for both Winnie and her siblings.

Portia would pretend to go to Winnie's house to ask after Batsi. While there, she would quickly collect the children's clothes and leave. Winnie would intercept the children on their way home to school and they would send them off in Portia brother's deliver lorry. Portia and Winnie would board along with their belongings and after dropping the children off at the aunt's house, Portia's brother would drive them to the nearest bus station to board the city bus.

* * *

It was three months since Winnie and Portia had successfully made their escapade. News had come from the village that Batsi had searched every house in the village for Tommy and Chipo. Ben on the other hand, had gone on a rampage accusing all the men in the village of assisting Winnie to escape so they would marry her.

Winnie had been able to know how her siblings were by means of writing letters.

Portia lived in a one bed roomed flat that was self-contained with every room easily accessible. The two girls shared the bedroom and they enjoyed sharing stories of Portia's work. She would tell Winnie of her boss, an English man named Gareth Walter. From the way Portia talked about him, he seemed to be a generous man who was easier to work with. Portia had taken Winnie to the town centre and she was so fascinated with the poles with changing lights that Portia said were traffic lights. Winnie had told a hysterical Portia that the town centre seemed to be a busy place and that it was amazing how people found food to eat without farming spaces. They were several aspects of the big city that fascinated Winnie. She always looked forward to weekends when Portia would take her out. Sometimes though, Portia had to work over time so that meant Winnie had to stay indoors. She did not feel confident to go out on her own.

Portia came back from work in the evening as usual. Winnie had spent the day cleaning and ironing .She greeted her friend with a broad smile, "hello Portia, you are welcome. How was your day?"

Portia warmly exchanged greetings with her dear friend who she had drawn closer to since they started living together.

After a supper of rice and beef stew, the two friends sat down and watched television.

Portia took the remote and switched off the TV. She turned to her friend who was sitting next to her and said, "I have some lovely news for you. My boss wants a cleaner for the offices and I quickly mentioned your name .what do you think?"

Winnie jumped up in excitement and held her swollen baby tummy, "Portia, thank you .oh thank you so much. Now I will afford to buy clothes for the baby."

"It's ok Winnie, I would have bought the things any way. It's only that you would do well with the extra cash, you know buying things for yourself and buying make up" Portia pretended to rub her face to emphasize her point. The girls sent off roaring with laughter.

Winnie stopped laughing and quietly said ", I would never get to the level you are Portia .Wearing all these makeup and looking lovely all the time. And that water you spray from the can, it smells sweet". Portia laughed at her friend's naivety. She said her good night and went to bed after instructing Winnie to get ready in the morning.

Early the next morning the two friends caught a bus to the city. The city was bustling with many busy serious looking people going to work. Winnie got used to this unfriendly environment. It was different from the village life where people greeted each other stranger or neighbour.

Winnie was wearing a white loose blouse and blue skirt and black shoes that Portia had given to her. She tied her long thick hair into a bun in the middle. Portia had applied some makeup and when Winnie had looked in the mirror, she could not believe the beautiful transformation.

As she walked next to Winnie, she felt a sense of importance wearing special clothes. By the time they got to the office, Winnie was more nervous of meeting Mr Walter. She had seen English people before at the village clinic were foreign doctors used to visit occasionally to educate the staff but she was not used to them.

The offices were airy and spacious .Portia sat behind the reception desk and pointed to a couch at the corner for her friend to sit on .Portia switched on what Winnie thought was a television, the only difference is that she seemed to be pressing buttons on a flat piece of equipment. Winnie watched in fascination at the technology.

After half an hour, a young English man walked through the office doors and spoke to Portia briefly who in turned and pointed in her direction. Gareth smiled broadly at Winnie and continued talking to Portia. He had a muscle built frame and the most sea blue eyes Winnie had ever seen. He had rustled sandy blonde hair and stubble of rough prickly beard that made him look manly. His teeth were white as milk. His cheekbones complemented his pointed nose and thin lips. Winnie was sure out of all the Englishmen she had met in the village this one was the most handsome.

Gareth walked into his office, and as soon as the door had shut behind them, Portia pointed at Winnie. "That is my boss. Did you see the way he is handsome? Can u imagine at his age he is not yet married. Rumor has it he is a bit of a ladies man. Anyway, you can go in for a brief interview. You will be fine" .Portia comforted her friend soothingly.

Winnie went into the office that had a big desk .Gareth was swivelling on a chair and had a pen on his lips. Winnie did not know what to do, whether to stand or sit. Everything was just too modern for her. Gareth seemed to sense her fear and invited her to sit on a chair opposite him. He offered her a cup of tea, which she politely declined for fear of embarrassing herself in case she did not like the taste of it.

.Gareth just grinned at her and made him self one. He coughed and started, "Winnie, that is your name right?"

Winnie nodded and Gareth continued, "Sorry I could not help to notice, are you pregnant?" Winnie still nodded.

Gareth shook his head and said, "Please feel free. Just talk its not formal .I really want to help you Winnie but I just feel uncomfortable to offer you this kind of a job. Especially in your condition. Our offices cover the whole floor and it might be too much for you .I will talk to Portia and think of something else you can do."

Winnie quickly knelt on the floor and begged, "Please, please Mr Walter. I am a strong woman. No need to worry about that .In the village, I worked men's jobs in this my condition. Cleaning is nothing, honestly, I need the job. I have a brother, a sister and a bab....."

"Please, please", Gareth pleaded, helping Winnie to her feet. "Don't kneel like that .I am just an ordinary person like you." He paused thoughtfully and continued, "I don't mean to pry, but what about your husband? Is he still in the village? Why not sent for him? I will rent him a room instead, employ him and you will sit at home and happy days!" Gareth finished, feeling satisfied for resolving the situation.

Winnie looked down on her lap and twiddled her fingers. She looked up again with watery eyes "; I do not have a husband. The man in the village is not my husband".

"Oh dear .Out of wedlock is it? When are you going to get married?"

"No Mr Walter .the man in the village raped me .I don't love him."

Gareth sat up, startled by the revelation the girl had made. He looked at her intently and asked, "What is he still doing in the village. Is he on bail? What nonsense! Giving him bail?"

Winnie shook her head and Gareth opened his mouth wide in amazement "what? You did not report him?"

"It is complicated sir," replied Winnie and she narrated the whole story. Gareth punched his fist on the desk. His face was tense and his eyes had turned icy, the warm look had disappeared. There was a long silence.

Gareth could not believe his ears. The girl in front of her was violated .she was the victim but the way she had been treated was worse than the offender himself was. He slammed his fist angrily on the desk and it made Winnie jump.

"Sorry", he apologised. "It just makes me mad knowing that they are some people who think they can get away with such types of crimes .Promise you Winnie, he will get his comeuppance. He shall pay. I can't believe this." He stood up and paced the office. At one point Winnie thought, she saw him dab a tear away.

"Winnie", he managed, with a whisper, "I do not want to pretend that I know what you are going through. All I know is that what you need now is definitely not a job. You need peace of mind. Rest and time out. You have had a horrible experience. It is important for you to know that not all this is your fault. What you went through in the village is persecution!" .He paused and swallowed hard. The warmth in his eyes returned and he continued, "Portia is a good lady. I know she has a heart of gold and I am glad she rescued you out of all this mess."

He took out wads of notes and handed it to a hesitant Winnie. "Please, take it. If I had a magic wand, I would undo all the sorrow and hurt you have gone through. I will get my driver to drive you back home. I will pass in a week's time hopefully Saturday. In addition, I will sit down with both of you women, and think how best you can educate yourself, and get a better job after the baby is born. Now I will help you financially. That is the best I can do." He shook his head in sadness and he was not convinced he had done much to help. Winnie knelt on the ground to thank him, only for Gareth to interrupt her.

Kevin and Katy had amended their relationship, especially when they found out that it was Kevin's cousins involved in the car jacking. Every month their relationship got stronger. Kevin always told Katy off if she misbehaved in any manner. Katy did not like it at first, but later began to enjoy it because she saw that Kevin was a genuine young man who wanted the best for her. She had even agreed not to report his cousins to the police on condition they pay the remaining of the money they had spend from the proceeds of selling her car.

Katy felt her relationship with her mother was improving because Kevin made sure she was in the house early and he had encouraged them both to quit smoking .He always said "lets not die young my dear"

Kevin respected her dignity, which Katy found strange at first. He always made sure that when they went out they were never in an isolated place. He even confessed that he feared temptation. Katy saw that beyond the "hard man" exterior laid a gentle and caring person.

Kevin encouraged her to call her brother to make amends to which she had said she was not ready but promised she would.

Andrea, her mother was getting frailer day by day. Katy knew that her mother was thinking of Gareth. She knew what she had to do to make her mother happy but she did not want to swallow her pride to be the first one to build the bridge.

She always imagined what had become of Gareth for the few months she had not seen him. Sometimes she felt she missed her big brother and other times she was glad he was out of their lives.

Kevin had advised Katy to start thinking of getting a job and to be more responsible. Kevin begun self-employment and ran his car mechanic business in front of his uncle's house. Katy hoped that one day she would be fortunate enough to get a job and make Kevin happy. That was her top priority.

That Saturday, Portia and Winnie woke up early and scrubbed the walls and the floor. Portia wanted to impress her boss with a clean house so he would know he had employed an organised person. They finished mid morning and slumped on the sofa. Portia heard the postman's bell outside her door and shouted, "Post man!"

Winnie and Portia raced to the door like little children. There was only one letter addressed to Winnie .Both girls looked at each in amazement. Who had the knowledge that both Winnie lived with Portia? Winnie hurriedly tore off the seal and the letter read:

Huyu village

Post office Box 56

Huyu

23 October 2006

Dear sister Winnie.

I hope you are doing well .I know you will be surprised on receiving this letter. At school, we have learnt a lot about writing letters and I felt the need to make my first practice on you. Tommy is fine. He enjoys going to school. Thank you very much for the money you and sister Portia sent to mama, we no longer call her aunty. She has been very kind to us. She always encourages us to focus on our education. We have someone who lives here and helps with work, in return, she gives us food and somewhere to sleep

I have sad news. Brother Batsi is not feeling well. Sister Portia's mother told mama who later informed us. They say he has lost a lot of weight and he has a running stomach that makes it impossible for him to eat anything.

We cannot go to see him in case he discovers were we live. We enjoy staying here .We also heard that Tracy is living with Ben but there is unconfirmed rumours that both of them are not feeling too well. I am sorry I had to break this news. Please sister I would love to come to the city. I heard they have tall buildings the same as our village mountain. One of my friends who have an aunt in the city told me that. I would love to see it for myself. Do you have a baby? If yes, name her after me.

Thank you sister and Tommy says hallo

We love you

Yours

Chipo

Winnie slowly folded the crispy paper and handed it to her friend. She sat back on the sofa slowly. She felt weak in her knees. Things were happening so fast. She was glad though that her siblings were fine. Her pain was her brother. Despite all the cruelty he put her through, she hurt for him. They had the same blood running in their veins.

Portia sat next to her friend and rubbed her shoulders gently. Immediately there was a gentle knock at the front of the door. Portia panicked .She did not know what to touch .she wanted everything perfect. Winnie saw that her friend was panicking and she took it on herself to open the door. Gareth stood at the entrance. Winnie smelt his fresh perfume and noticed that he had shaved off the scruffy beard. They exchanged greetings and he handed Winnie a couple of big brown bags that were full of clothes and other fashion accessories.

Portia greeted her boss and went into the kitchen to prepare food. For a moment, both of them sat in awkward silence. Gareth broke the silence

"Have you been to the nice places in the city Winnie?" Gareth asked.

"I have been to the town centre with Portia and I think it's really beautiful", Winnie shyly replied.

"Really? That is nice. What about a hotel?" For a moment, Gareth thought he had said something wrong because Winnie looked scared.

"A hotel, sir?"

Gareth unsurely replied, "Yes"

"That is were the important people go .I would never dream of going into a hotel sir."

Gareth chuckled, "Who told you that, anyone can eat in a hotel. Including you. All that is needed is the money .Winnie, please don't call me sir .It makes me feel old .I am only 32 years old." He shouted, "Portia!"

"Yes Gary" Portia replied.

Winnie was amazed at hearing her friend calling her boss by his first name. It was different from the office were she addressed him formally as "mister"

"Portia, please don't cook for me and Winnie. I think it is high time our friend here gets city baptised. She needs to know how people enjoy life. Do you want to come?" Gareth asked Portia who was now standing at the kitchen doorway.

"No thanks". Portia smiled. "You guys go ahead .I have a party to attend anyway. Come on Winnie lets get you changed".

Winnie stood up, not sure what she ton expect. She could not catch up with the city life events. To her, everyone was always in a rush and panicky. She needed time to digest the contents of the letter but she did not want to be rude to Gareth. He had been so helpful and concerned ever since she had told him about her experience.

Gareth handed the bags of clothes to Portia adding that all the stuff belonged to Winnie. Portia jumped around excitedly, pulling her friend towards the bedroom. A few minutes later, Winnie emerged from the bedroom. Gareth could hardly recognise her. Standing in front of him was the most naturally beautiful woman he had come across. Her hair was loose on the shoulders and her face was silky smooth. He had bought a maternity long dress with stripped patterns. He could not believe how it suited her. She was wearing sandals and the earrings, bracelet and necklace matched.

"Well?" Portia asked, impressed at the makeover she had done on her friend.

Gareth struggled to speak then slowly composed himself, "Well, wow. Ladies…I don't know what to say … I guess I have to say, my lady your coach awaits." Gareth was more struck at the innocence that Winnie had. She was a shy person and did not speak much. Gareth pinched himself to reality.

The car journey to the hotel was excessively comfortable. Winnie concluded that by sitting in Gareth car it was the same as sitting in an aeroplane. She could not hear the sound of the engine. The music was soft and soothing. She relaxed her head on the headrest and enjoyed the drive. From the corner of her eye, she could see Gareth stealing glances at her.

Chapter 7

When they walked into the hotel lobby, Winnie felt overwhelmed by the beauty of it. They were decorated lights all over the ceiling. Tall flowers and plants were stationed on every corner and the floor was polished she could see her own reflection. Never had she seen a place so clean like that .The people who worked there walked in a similar professional way. It was obvious that Gareth was popular at the hotel because all the hotel workers greeted him cheerfully. The waiter led them to a table.

Winnie followed Gareth sheepishly. She wanted to turn around and take to her heels but the obvious fact was she did not know where she was.

The place was too beautiful for her that she felt she could not be a part of it. Gareth turned around and took her hand into his. Winnie felt a lot calmer. At the table, there were many utensils. The only ones she recognised were the fork, knife and spoon. She had seen them at Portia's house. The other utensils were strange shapes and well polished. The waiter pulled a chair for her and assisted Winnie to sit down.

She noticed Gareth was used to the lifestyle with the way he picked up a card that had food drawn on and big letters written "MENU". They were other people who looked important and were occupying other tables. Moreover, they were concentrating on the food or whispering to each other.they did not seem to mind the people around them. The room was unusually calm and not noisy. There was soft music, same as the one that Gareth had played in his car on their way there.

After looking through Gareth passed the card to Winnie. She did not know what to do with it. He urged her to browse through and choose anything she wanted, no matter how unfamiliar it was. Winnie could not make out the words on the card. They were complicated .She pointed to Gareth on the one written "fish". She wanted to stay within her comfort zone and fish was the only familiar word she saw.

The waiter bought some weird shaped glasses, which had water for her beer for Gareth. Gareth had a sip and nodded in satisfaction. Winnie sipped on her water and spat it out. It was icy cold! Gareth laughed loudly and handed an ashamed Winnie a napkin to dry herself. He called for the waiter and instructed him to fetch tap water.

Winnie felt at ease on noticing that Gareth was not angry with him.

While waiting for the food, Gareth told Winnie about England. How beautiful it was and that snow fell in winter. Winnie was surprised. Flakes of ice falling from the sky were too unimaginable for Winnie to comprehend. She shivered at the thought. She noticed that Gareth was a humble person who no doubt he was rich, did not mind to mingle with a poor person like her. She felt happy as Gareth told jokes and reminisced about the past.

When the food arrived, Winnie stared at her plate in amazement. There was no fish on the plate. The food was made of green vegetables, diced white cubes and swirly things that she could not make out what they were.

"Oh, what's the matter Winnie? You do not like your food. Dont worry you can order some more." Gareth quipped gently while looking around for a waiter.

Winnie felt ashamed at her lack of manners and quickly said, "No sir... err Gareth.It's only that I asked for fish and it is not on my plate. It is all right, I can eat this. It's still hotel food"

Winnie impressed Gareth with innocent character. He pulled the plate towards him and said "its fish alright .you see these white bits? That is the fish .they skin it off, take away the bones and cut it into these shapes and this is pasta. It is wheat. Good choice" he winked at Winnie and passed the plate back to her.

Winnie looked at Gareth and tried to copy the way he was using the fork and knife. The more she tried the more the pasta fell on the table. She could not hide her shame. Gareth took his own fork, picked a few of the pasta and fed them to her.Winnie embarrassingly chewed on the food and thought she would not blame Gareth if he did not bring her again to wonderful places because of the humiliation she caused that night .

Gareth though, was impressed at the way Winnie tried to adjust to the comfortable lifestyle. He saw her determination to try at the same time being honest with her failure. He told her to use the fork because it was much easier. He dropped the knife and used the fork. Their eyes met and they both burst out in laughter. It was the first time that Gareth had been genuinely happy. The last time he remembered was when his father was still alive.

He was very glad that he still had happiness left in him.

The evening went well and Winnie was getting used to the environment and ordered some ice cream. Gareth laughed out every time she screwed her face when she ate the cold ice cream. She enjoyed the taste though it was freezing her teeth. Gareth paid the bill and he offered to drop her back home.Winnie felt secure and comfortable for the first time in her life. She wished life would always be like that permanently.

It had been almost five moths since Andrea had talked to her son. Her relationship with her daughter Katy had improved. Andrea was struggling to eat or sleep. The thought of her family scattered hurt her. Every time she took the phone, dialled Gareth's number and she would cut the line off. She kept making excuses to herself, blaming the incident.

The doctor had expressed concern over her gaunt unhealthy frame. He had advised she had to sort whatever that was worrying her.

It was a dry afternoon and there were sunny spells .Andrea sat on the porch of her house. It faced the front garden. She usually sat there whenever she needed to refresh her mind.

The automatic gates opened. Andrea was surprised because she was not expecting anybody and Katy had stayed home the whole day.

She almost dropped her jaws when she saw her son's car pulling into the driveway. Andrea stood up and walked over to the entrance of the porch. Gareth came out of the car and a pregnant Winnie emerged from the passenger's side. For a moment, Andrea stood in her tracks, staring at Winnie.She decided to continue welcoming the visitors, and hid her surprise.

Gareth offered his hand to his mother.Andrea pulled in her son, and sobbed whilst holding him close.Gareth held on to his mother too and blinked back tears.Winnie stood by ,watching.

Andrea ushered them both into the house.

"Katy's sleeping." Andrea sniffed and wiped her tears.

Gareth smiled at his mother effortlessly then said, "Really? That is a first .Katy staying at home! Is she not feeling well?"

"She is fine. She decided to spend the day with me." Andrea explained to a stunned Gareth and continued, "Yes, your sister has really changed. Ever since she met a young man called Kevin, she has been so well behaved."

Gareth found it hard to believe that his sister had the capacity to listen to anyone. He found it very intriguing that he told his mother he wanted to meet Kevin and show his gratitude.

.He turned his attention to Winnie and introduced her to his mother, "Mum, this lovely lady here is Winnie. She is a very dear friend of mine."

Andrea did not respond, she stood up and walked towards the kitchen were she called out. "Gareth please come over here and help me make some refreshments".

Gareth did so, and stood next to the fridge watching his frail mother open the cupboards for glasses. He felt sorry for her.

There was an awkward silence in the kitchen and the only sound was the clinking of the glasses.Gareth rubbed his hands excitedly and asked his mother, "So mum what do you think?"

"Of what?" Andrea snapped irritably.

"Of the girl, you know Winnie?"

Andrea put on her reading glasses as a destruction method. She did not know how to react to the news she dreaded to receive. "What about her? I thought you said she is a dear friend?"

Gareth paced excitedly ", yes mum... yes... but I want to ...I want to ask her hand in marriage ... she is a nice girl mum... well mannered, beautiful a...."

"Gareth!" his mother cut in ", you have made the girl pregnant already out of wedlock! You have put shame on the family and yourself .The only thing to do is marry her. Why did you not come with her before she was pregnant and asked for my opinion then?" Andrea continued pouring juice in the glasses. Her face was thunder with anger.

"Mother, please may you calm down. It's not like that," Gareth explained to his mother who stopped what she was doing and faced him. He swallowed deeply, "I did not make her pregnant."

Andrea chuckled sarcastically, "I am an old woman, keep up with me. You want to marry her but you are denying her pregnancy?"

"Well" Gareth was short of words at first, then continued, "Well, mum, its a long story...I want to marry her .She does not know that .I have fallen for her and I want to be family with her before the baby is born ,to make it all normal.. No, mum it is not my pregnancy. I met her when she was pregnant already."

Gareth jumped at the sound of the counter banging. His mother had slammed so hard that she was fighting to catch her breath. Before he could say more, she splashed juice on him, "Are you mad? How about flying back to England and get someone your own calibre? To top it all, you get a ready-made pregnant girl. Do you want to kill me? Is this the end of the Walter name? What will people say? Please reverse that decision or I will disown you."

Mother and son squared to each other, both fuming. Gareth brushed off at his wet shirt and slowly growled, "I love you mum and I will not be tempted to have an argument with you, I am a grown man .I make my own decisions. I only came here to let you know out of respect. Mum, I can go ahead and marry her. No one and I repeat no one will stop me."

"Oh really?" Andrea snarled back. "Is that why you came back to show me that you are making a fool out of yourself once more?"

"Mum, I am here because Winnie persuaded me to come. You had said you would call me in your own time when you were ready .I guess I should have waited because you are clearly not ready."

Gareth stormed out of the kitchen and left a frustrated Andrea panting. He grabbed his jacket from the sofa and helped a confused Winnie up, "Come on Winnie .Let's get out of here".

Katy watched from her bedroom window as her brother reversed the car and sped out the gate towards the road.

She went to the kitchen and saw her mother sitting on one the chairs, her head down. "Mum". Katy whispered.

"I guess you heard that entire fracas? Your brother again"

"I did mum and I think as a matter of fact you were too harsh on Gary."

Andrea looked questionably at Katy .She was always opposed to her brother's ideas.

"Yes mum". Katy sat down opposite her and held her hands into her. "He is an adult .A heart is like a tree mum, it grows wherever it likes."

"Are you sure you are alright Katy?" Andrea checked.

"I am fine mum. It is only that my boyfriend Kevin educated me on appreciating people in my life. His own mother was a village girl who got married to the farmer's son .The family was from the Netherlands. Kevin does not have a clear memory of his father. You know why mum?" Andrea shook her head and listened intently to her daughter.

"Well, because of this very kind of attitude. Kevin's grandfather left the farm with all his family including his father because of the shame on his family.Kevin's mum died, and his life spiralled into oblivion. He had to fight for survival. I am personally ashamed for the excuses I used to get my way because I grew up without daddy. I recognised my problems were much more insignificant compared to Kevin"

Katy stood up and pushed the chair "Mum, if you want Gareth to be part of the family, embrace that girl and her unborn child. Gareth regards that child as his own, let it be. Would you lose a son for being snobbish? Look at you mum. It is obvious you are not well, because you miss him. If you do not embrace the girl he loves, you stand to lose him. This time forever. Good day mum" she bent and kissed her mother on the forehead and went over to the fridge to fetch water. Andrea was gobsmacked to notice a truly transformed woman in her daughter.

Winnie had hesitated when Gareth made his intentions of marrying her known .She felt she was not worth to be his wife. She had asked him relentlessly what he had seen in her that he had not seen in other girls. Gareth had convinced her that he loved her despite any situation. Winnie had confided in her friend Tracy who encouraged to feel fortunate she had a man who would take her and her unborn child.

Winnie deeply loved Gareth for his kindness and the way he made her feel happy and secure.

The wedding day arrived and Portia's house was buzzing with colleagues who had come to see the bride and those involved with making the bride beautiful. Winnie's sister and brother were there too and Gareth had agreed to let them stay with the couple after the wedding.

Winnie sat on the chair facing the mirror and her face was solemn. Portia walked in the bedroom holding a tiara. She was happy for the couple and she sang loudly on top of her voice. She went over to her friend, adjusted her hair, and inserted some pearl pins. "If I did not know you I would think you are getting cold feet. However, I know the way you love Gareth. What is wrong, why the face?"

Winnie sighed deeply, "I am happy I am getting married Portia. Any girl would, do you know that I have to pinch my self to make sure I am not dreaming. It is just months ago, I was in a situation that was a matter of live or die. Look at me now. Do I deserve this?"

Portia touched her friend's shoulders, and then said, "You know what, look in the mirror .Think, are you not looking at a stunning woman? When growing up you were the girl my mother always used an example on us whenever we were naughty. You are someone to cherish. What is wrong if Gareth wants to be the one to cherish you?"

Winnie sighed deeply and smiled, "Why me? Look at my state. I am pregnant with someone's child"

"So? Will you be pregnant forever? Is it not the same as meeting a man when you have the child? In addition, remember the circumstances you got the child under .Today is one of the happiest days of your life. You are getting married to the most handsome and kind hearted person I know .Cheer up and get dressed"

The girls met their gazes in the mirror and burst out laughing. They hugged each other, continued applying make up, and making final adjustments to the dress and tiara.

"Portia, visitors!" a voice called out.

"Oh dear, my hands are full at the moment, who could it be? We will be late for the service". Portia half talked to Winnie then called out, "In the bedroom. The visitor may enter please."

The girls continued working away on the preparations. The door opened slowly and a head peered in. It was Andrea.

Winnie caught her breath. Her heart skipped a beat as she wondered if Gareth's mother had come to stop the wedding. To her amazement, Andrea walked in, leant over, and kissed her on the cheek.

"You look beautiful, the bride of the century". Andrea said as she wiped off the lipstick mark she had left on Winnie's cheek.

Behind her, was Katy who smiled and waved to Winnie and Portia.

"Stand up and give us a twirl"Andrea said turning her finger around to gesture her point.

Winnie stood up and twirled as the women in the room gave their approvals. The design of the white dress was simple with a few pearls around the bodice. Her pregnancy did not draw any attention in the beautiful dress. Her hair was straight with spirals at the front and the tiara sat perfectly on her hair. She had little foundation that made her skin chocolaty brown and the turquoise eye shadow was subtle yet made her big eyes more beautiful. Her lips were in bronze shade. She looked immaculate and exquisite.

Andrea gave her daughter in law a cuddle and slowly started, "I have learnt one thing in life. To appreciate people the way they are. I am sorry for the rudeness that I displayed when you came with my son. I thought he deserved better, after seeing you, there is no more I can wish for my son. And besides it was high time he settled". The women laughed at the comment.

Andrea continued, "It does not matter that your own mother is dead .I am your mother now. I take you as my own and I will be much closer to you because my own daughters will be married to other families." Andrea comforted a teary Winnie. "Don't cry child .Focus on the future now. Bad experiences happen in life, we have to move on. I have a present for you." She dipped her hand in the bag and brought out tickets "These are tickets to England for your honeymoon once the baby is born and I know Gareth would love to visit and show you off to our friends and relatives. Welcome to the family Winnie". Andrea gave Winnie another cuddle and there was no dry eye in the room, as everyone got emotional.

Later after the wedding, Gareth and his wife relaxed on the sofa and shared a bottle of wine. The fireplace was on and warm.

Gareth pulled Winnie closer and kissed her tenderly, "We have to move out of this small place as soon as the baby is born."

"And the family is expanded. That is a great idea".Winnie replied tenderly.

Gareth sipped on his wine and said, "I am glad the wedding went well and mum attended. Finally, I met the man responsible for the new Katy. I like him, I would not mind playing golf with him next week".

Gareth noticed his wife was deep in thought "What's wrong baby? You seem too distant."

"Well", Winnie said, "I am thinking of my brother Batsi.Portia's mother told me today at the wedding reception that he is like a walking skeleton".

"Ummm, how do you want us to help sweetie?"

"Well if it is not too much trouble I would love for him to be admitted to the nearest village hospital and I would visit him after the baby is born."

Gareth stroked the baby bump and said, "Of course my love, your wish is my command I will sort it out straight away."

"Thank you." Winnie appreciated.

"Now, what I can't wait for is our little bay to be born and we will be a proper little family. Winnie I love you and I am glad you are in my life. Thank you for being my wife."

"No, thank you for being my husband .If anyone had told me that I would get married to a person like you, I would tell them to stop wishful thoughts. To you I owe for restoring my dignity."

With that, Winnie held her husband's hand closely to her heart.

THE END